by BERNARD WABER

IRA SAYS GOODBYE

Houghton Mifflin Company, Boston 1988

for Dara, Aaron, Tamra and Jarad

Library of Congress Cataloging-in-Publication Data

Waber, Bernard.
    Ira says goodbye.

    Summary: Ira is surprised to discover that his best
friend Reggie feels happy about having to move to a new
town.
    [1. Moving, Household—Fiction. 2. Friendship—
Fiction] I. Title.
PZ7.W113Iq   1988   [E]   88-6823
ISBN 0-395-48315-8

Printed in the United States of America

Y   10 9 8 7 6 5 4 3 2 1

Reggie, my best friend,
was moving away.
My sister was the first
to tell me about it.
This is how she told me.
She said:

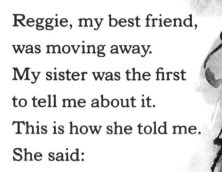

"I . . . ra . . . !"

"What?" I said.

"Do I have a surprise for you!"

(I knew, right away, I would
hate the surprise).

"What?" I said.

"What I just heard."

(I knew, right away, I shouldn't
say *what* again).

"What?" I said again.
"Guess," she said.

"GOODBYE!" I said.
"Wait!" she said.

"Somebody is going to
be doing something."
"What?" I said.
"Real soon."
"What?" I said.
"Something."

"GOODBYE!" I said.
"Wait!" she said.

"Moving," she said.
"Somebody is moving?" I said.
"In two weeks."
"Who?" I said.
"Aren't you going to guess?"
"Whoooooooooooo?" I said.
"Not even one little,
teenie, tiny guess?"

7

"GOODBYE!" I said.

"Wait!" she said.

"Reggie!"
"What!" I said.
"Your best friend."
"Is moving?"
"Away," she said. "Far, far away. Oh, I
would hate it to pieces if my best friend
were moving away. What will you do
when your best friend in the whole wide world
moves away? Hmmmmmm?"

"I don't believe it," I said.
"Believe it," she said.

I ran into the house.

"It's true," said my mother.

"We were just coming to tell you," said my father.

"We learned about it only minutes ago," said my mother.

"But it's not as though you won't ever see Reggie again," said my father. "Greendale is only an hour's drive."

"Greendale?" I said.

"Where Reggie will be living," said my mother.

"And you can always talk on the telephone," said my father.

"But talking on the telephone won't be the same," I said.

"I know," said my mother.

"I know," said my father.

Reggie, moving!
I couldn't believe it.
Reggie was my best friend
as far back as I could remember.
We had our own tree house

and a secret
hiding place
that only we knew about
because it was so secret.

And we had a magic act:
the Amazing Reggie
and the Fantastic Ira.
Everyone came
to see us perform.

And we had our own club:
The Dolphins.
So far, there were only two members — us.
But we thought it was a good start.

I went to all of Reggie's
birthday parties.
And he came to all of mine.

We put our baseball cards
together, so that way
it would make a bigger pile.

When Reggie was
away on vacation,
I took care of
his dog, Herman.
He did the same
for Geraldine,
my cat.

And when Reggie was
sick in the hospital,
I sent him
a get-well card.
I made it myself.

And when I was away,
visiting my grandparents
in Oregon, Reggie sent me
a miss-you card.

We even put our turtles together
in the same tank, so they could be
best friends too — like us.
My turtle was Felix.
His was Oscar.

I decided to go and find Reggie,
and tell him how sorry I felt
to hear he was moving away.

I found Reggie.
We both started talking
at the same time.
"You're moving," I said.
"We're moving," he said.
"To Greendale," I said.
"To Greendale," he said.
And then he said,
"My father has a new job."
"In Greendale," I said.

Reggie sighed.
I sighed too.
"We can still talk on
the telephone," I said.
"But that won't be the same,"
said Reggie.
"I know," I said.

But the next day, to my surprise,
Reggie wasn't the same Reggie anymore.
"Isn't it terrible?" I said.
"Isn't it terrific?" he said.
I looked at Reggie. "Did you just
say terrific?"
"Uh-huh," said Reggie.
"Did you just say uh-huh?" I said.
"Uh-huh," said Reggie.

I couldn't believe it.
I said to Reggie, "When you just
said uh-huh, the way you just
said uh-huh, did you mean
— uh-huh — you're glad you're moving?"
"Uh-huh," said Reggie.

Reggie started to explain: "Greendale is going to
be so great," he said. "Great, great, great!
My father told me all about it — last night.
In Greendale, all people do is have fun. Fun, fun, fun,
all of the time. Listen to this:
There's this place in Greendale where they keep
this killer shark. Every day, people go to this place
to see this killer shark — just so they can get scared.
Because the minute this killer shark sees everybody,
he starts to snort."

"Sharks snort?" I said.

"This one snorts," said Reggie. "And he makes killer shark faces at everybody, because that's what killer sharks love best to do, make ugly, scary killer shark faces at people. Isn't that great!"

"And do you know what else about Greendale?" said Reggie. "There's this park, with games and thriller rides. And all people do all day, in Greendale, is play these games, and scream their heads off riding these thriller rides — and watch fireworks Saturday nights. Isn't that great!"

"And do you know what else about Greendale?" said Reggie. "There's this lake, with swans and ducks, and cute little baby swans and ducks too. And the minute these swans and ducks see you coming, they just scoot right up to you, just so you can feed them. Isn't that great!"

"And the people in Greendale are so friendly," said Reggie. "All they do, all day long, is go around smiling. Smiling, smiling, smiling, all of the time. They just never get tired of smiling. And they give you this big hello, no matter how many times they see you. Even if they see you two hundred times a day, they'll stop and say hello. Isn't that great!"

"People here are friendly," I said.

"Some are even best friends."

But Reggie just went on talking about Greendale, as if
he had never heard about best friends.
"Oh, I almost forgot the most terrific part," said Reggie,
"the part about my Uncle Steve. He plays football for the
Greendale Tigers, you know. And I'll be seeing him every day.
And he's going to teach me to kick and pass, so that when
I grow up, I'll play football for the Greendale Tigers too.
Isn't that great!"

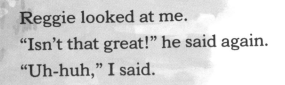

Reggie looked at me.
"Isn't that great!" he said again.
"Uh-huh," I said.

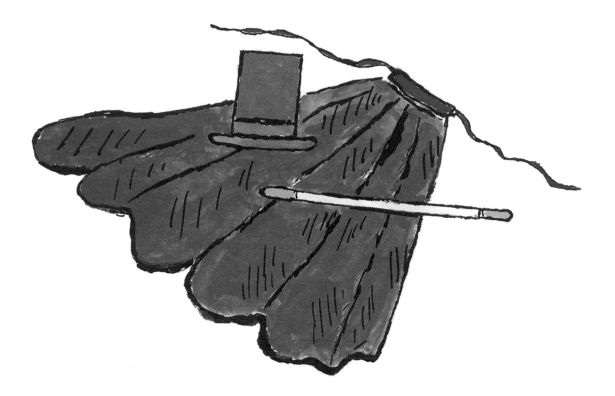

Day after day, Reggie had new stories to tell about Greendale.
He never seemed to want to do any of our old things anymore,
like going up to the tree house or performing the magic act.
He even took back his top hat, cape, and wand, which were kept
at the secret hiding place.
And while he was at it, he took his baseball cards.
It was as if Reggie had already moved away.

One day, Reggie came by to take back Oscar, his turtle.
It was my turn to keep the tank.
"But Felix and Oscar are friends," I said. "They're
used to being together."
"They're only turtles," said Reggie.
"Turtles have feelings," I said. "And nobody can explain
to a turtle why his friend isn't with him anymore."
"Nothing bothers turtles," said Reggie.
"Turtles are bothered. They're bothered a whole lot,"
I said. "Turtles get lonely. And they get sad — especially
if a friend is taken away. And they start to mope."

"Turtles do not mope," said Reggie.

"They do so mope," I said. "Everybody knows that. And they stop eating. And they get sick — even die. Do you want that to happen, Reggie?"

"They don't die," said Reggie, "not from losing a friend."

"They do, too, die," I said. "Everybody knows that about turtles. Everybody who isn't stupid knows that."

"I'm taking Oscar," said Reggie.

"Then take Felix, too," I said.

Reggie looked at me. "Do you mean it?" he said.

"Uh-huh," I said.

And that's just what happened.
Reggie walked out with Oscar —
and Felix.

Maybe I shouldn't have said that part about being stupid.

But sometimes Reggie gets to me.

Sometimes Reggie really gets to me.

Like whenever I call Reggie on the telephone,

and I say to him, "What are you doing?"

He always says, "Talking to you" — like I didn't

know he was talking to me.

I can't tell you how many times he pulled that one.

Do you want to know something else about Reggie?
When Reggie eats lunch, he always laughs with his mouth
wide open, and with all that yuckie food showing.
I hate that about Reggie.

And Reggie doesn't care one bit about friends.
He really doesn't.
He didn't care one bit how lonely
Felix and Oscar would feel
without each other.

Do you want to know something?
I just hope some new kid moves into Reggie's old house;
some new kid who will be my best friend;
some new kid who won't always be bragging about
his uncle the football player.
Do you want to know something else?
I can't wait for Reggie to move.
Do you want to know something else?
I will jump for joy
the day Reggie moves away.

I didn't have to wait long.

One day, a big van pulled up to Reggie's house.

I watched as the men carried everything

out of the house.

When the house was empty,
Reggie and his parents came outside.
Reggie was carrying the tank
with Felix and Oscar in it.
My parents and sister were there too.
Everyone hugged and said goodbye —
everyone except Reggie and me.

"Aren't you two going to say
goodbye?" said Reggie's mother.

Suddenly, Reggie burst out crying and couldn't stop.

He cried and cried, and no amount of patting seemed to help.

"Reggie is taking this move so hard," said his father.

At last, when Reggie stopped crying,
he handed me the tank.
He said, "Here, Ira, you keep them."
"You're giving Felix and Oscar to me?" I said.
"Uh-huh," said Reggie.
I was so surprised.

I dug into my pocket for my baseball cards,
and handed Reggie the one I always knew he wanted.
"You're giving me your favorite card!" said Reggie.
"Uh-huh," I said.
This time it was Reggie's turn to be surprised.

We all waved goodbye as Reggie and his parents drove away.
When their car disappeared, we looked at each other.
Everyone was sad.
"There's only one thing to do at a time like this,"
said my mother.
"What?" I said.
"Let's go into the house and bake a cake."
"Excellent," said my father.
"What kind of cake?" said my sister.
"How about angel food?" said my mother.

And that's just what we did,
the day Reggie moved.
We baked a cake.

That night, the telephone rang.

"It's for you, Ira," said my father.

It was Reggie. "What are you doing?" he said.

"Talking to you," I said.

"Stop fooling," said Reggie.

"I'm eating cake," I said.

"Listen," said Reggie, "would you like to
visit at my house this weekend? My father
and I can pick you up."

"Oh, would I!" I said. "Will your uncle Steve
be there?"

"Uh-huh," said Reggie.

"Great!" I said. "I can't wait."

"Just a minute," said Reggie. "My mother
wants to ask your mother if it's all right
for you to come."

My mother got on the telephone.

"Say yes," I whispered.

"Yes . . . I mean . . . hello!
Oh, hello, Ellie!"

Ellie is Reggie's mother.

"How are things?" said my mother.

"Say yes," I whispered.

My mother said, "Uh-huh." And then she said
some more "uh-huhs." And then she said, "Yes.
Yes, yes, yes," she kept saying.

Yes, yes, yes, I kept shaking my head.

And then she said, "Oh, won't that be nice!"

I knew what she meant by "nice."

"It will be very nice," I whispered.

"You're sure it won't be trouble?" she said.

"It won't be trouble," I shook my head.

"Saturday." My mother looked at me
hugging myself.

"I know he'll be delighted," she said.

My mother hung up.

"Guess what?" she said.

"I'm invited to Reggie's house," I called out,
as I ran up the stairs.

"Ira, where are you rushing to?" said my father.

"Up to pack," I said.

"But you're not leaving until Saturday," said
my mother. "You have two whole days to pack."

"I don't want to be late," I said.